Tana Hoban

Is It Larger? Is It Smaller?

Greenwillow Books
An Imprint of HarperCollinsPublishers

Library of Congress Cataloging-in-Publication Data
Hoban, Tana.   Is it larger? Is it smaller?
"Greenwillow Books."
Summary: Photographs of animals and objects in larger
and smaller sizes suggest comparisons between the two.
ISBN 0-688-15287-2 (pbk.)
1. Size perception—Juvenile literature.   [1. Size.]   I. Title.
BF299.S5H63   1985   84-13719   132.1'42
12 13 SCP 20 19 18 17 16 15 14 13 12 11

THIS ONE IS

FOR MY FATHER

WHO TOLD ME

I WAS WONDERFUL